The Frightened Kitten

Also by Holly Webb:
Max the Missing Puppy
Ginger the Stray Kitten
Buttons the Runaway Puppy
Little Puppy Lost

The Frightened Kitten

by Holly Webb
Illustrated by Sophy Williams

tiger tales

For Lara

tiger tales

5 River Road, Suite 128, Wilton, CT 06897
Published in the United States 2015
Originally published in Great Britain 2012
by Little Tiger Press
Text copyright © 2012 Holly Webb
Illustrations copyright © 2012 Sophy Williams
ISBN-13: 978-1-58925-465-7
ISBN-10: 1-58925-465-1
Printed in China
All rights reserved.

10 9 8 7 6 5 4 3 2

For more insight and activities, visit us at www.tigertalesbooks.com

Chapter One

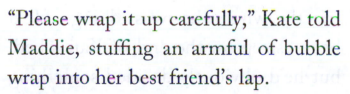

"Please wrap it up carefully," Kate told Maddie, stuffing an armful of bubble wrap into her best friend's lap.

Maddie nodded, winding it around the picture frame. "Shadow looks handsome in this picture," she said, her voice a little shaky.

Kate nodded. "He always does. But that's my favorite picture of him."

Maddie stared down at the photo. She was in it, too. It had been taken last summer, and showed Kate and her, with Kate's huge black cat, Shadow, sitting on the rug between them. He was almost as tall as they were when the girls were sitting down.

Maddie laughed with surprise as a hard head butted her arm, and Shadow stomped his way on to her lap to see exactly what she was doing. He'd been asleep on the end of Kate's bed, but he'd obviously decided something interesting was happening. He was the world's nosiest cat.

"Do you think he'll mind moving?" Maddie asked, watching Kate fill a cardboard box with books and her trinkets, all carefully wrapped up.

"I don't know. " Kate shrugged. "The new house has a big yard, but he likes it here. Like me." She sighed miserably. "I keep hoping Dad's going to come home and say it was all a mistake, and he doesn't have to go and work in Chicago after all. But we're leaving tomorrow. It's getting a little late for that." She sniffed, and sat down next to Maddie and Shadow.

Maddie put an arm around her, and Shadow bounced onto Kate's lap, standing up on his hind legs to wrap his front paws around her neck. It was his trick. Kate always told people she had a cat who hugged, although he didn't do it to very many people. Mostly Kate, but he would do it to Maddie sometimes, especially if she'd given him a cat treat. He'd even done it to Maddie's dad once, when he came to pick Maddie up. Her dad had been surprised, but Maddie had noticed that he always looked for Shadow whenever he came to Kate's now. As though he was hoping that Shadow might do it again.

Maddie had been working on her mom and dad to let her get a cat of her own for a while. She was pretty sure that Shadow had won her dad over that day. Now she just had to persuade her mom....

Kate sniffed again. "What if he doesn't like the new house, Maddie? He might even try and find his way back here. You read in the papers about cats who do that."

"Chicago's probably too far for him to try it," Maddie said. It was meant to be comforting, but it didn't work. She didn't want to think about how far away her friend was going to be. And she was going to have to start a new school, of course. Maddie couldn't imagine having to do that.

Kate frowned. "I hope there aren't too many other cats near the new house.

Shadow's the top cat around here. None of the other cats would put a paw in our yard. But the new yard might be another cat's territory already."

Maddie looked down at Shadow, now sitting on Kate's lap. He yawned and stretched, and then stared up at her with huge green eyes. *He* didn't look like he was worried.

"Even if the yard is another cat's territory, I don't think it will be for long," Maddie said, petting him.

Kate nodded, laughing. "Maybe. He doesn't fight very often, but when he does, I think he just sits on the other cats and squashes them." She sighed. "I'd better finish packing. Mom says I should have had it finished yesterday." She pushed Shadow gently off her knee, and he slunk away to hide among the boxes.

Maddie went back to wrapping up the photo. She was going to miss Kate so much. She knew Kate would miss her, too, but her friend was a bit like Shadow, Maddie thought. She was so strong and confident. She'd have a new group of friends in no time, and she'd be showing off her famous hugging cat to them instead.

"Please pass me that tape, Maddie, so I can seal this box up."

Maddie handed her the packing tape, then wrapped another picture frame. "Where did Shadow go?" she asked, a few minutes later.

"He's under the bed, isn't he?" Kate said, peering down.

But he wasn't. There was a sudden thumping and then a muffled yowl. "He's in the box!" Maddie giggled.

Kate stared at the big cardboard box she'd just taped up. "He can't be...." she said, but she didn't sound very sure. She ripped off the tape, and the flaps came up, followed by a large black head, with angry, glowing green eyes. The cat scrambled out, hissing grumpily.

"Well, you shouldn't have been in there!" Kate laughed. "Nosy boy!"

Maddie was laughing, too. But even as she laughed, she was thinking, *I'm going to miss them so much....*

Kate and her mom walked Maddie home — it was a beautiful day, warm and sunny. Perfect Easter vacation weather. If Kate hadn't been leaving tomorrow, they'd have spent time in the park, or maybe gone out somewhere for the day.

"Those cats that live next door to you are nearly as big as Shadow," Kate's mom commented as they came up to Maddie's yard.

"They're sitting on Mom's daffodils again," Maddie sighed, as she tried to shoo the two big tabby cats off the stone pot that her mom had planted full of bulbs. For some reason, Tiger and Tom had decided it was a really good place to sit and take a nap, and the daffodils were looking a little squashed now.

Maddie's mom opened the front door. "I heard you coming, girls. Oh, no, not those awful cats again!"

Tiger spat angrily at Maddie as she got him off the daffodils. He was so different from sweet-natured Shadow. At last, he jumped down, and the two of them stalked away, glaring back at Maddie.

As the moms talked, Kate flung her arms around Maddie. "Promise you'll call me every day! Tell me everything that's happening at school, okay?"

Maddie nodded. "You're coming back to visit at Christmas break."

"We'd better go," Kate's mom said. "It'll be a long day tomorrow, and there's still some packing to do."

And that was it. Kate and her mom went back down the path, waving, and Maddie was left on her own.

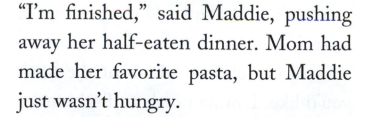

"I'm finished," said Maddie, pushing away her half-eaten dinner. Mom had made her favorite pasta, but Maddie just wasn't hungry.

15

Her dad leaned over and put an arm around her shoulders. "Do you think we could tell her the news? To cheer her up?" he suggested to Maddie's mom, and she nodded.

"What news?" Maddie sniffed sadly.

"Do you remember I told you that my friend Donna's cat had kittens a couple of months ago?" Mom asked.

"Oh, yes. You showed me a picture. They're beautiful. There were some tortoiseshell ones – my favorite kind!"

"Good. Because one of them is going to be yours!"

Maddie blinked. "I'm getting a kitten?"

"You can choose which of the litter you'd like. Donna needs to find homes for them all, and we thought it would be nice for you to have a cat, since you've wanted one for so long. And especially since you're going to miss Kate. Getting to know a kitten might make things less sad." Her mom looked at her anxiously. "We're not trying to take your mind off of missing her, Maddie. It's a really sad thing for a friend to move away."

"It just seemed like a good time," her dad added.

Maddie nodded. "It *is* a good time," she whispered. She couldn't help feeling sad about Kate, of course, but at the same time, inside she was bubbling with excitement. *A kitten! A kitten! I'm getting a kitten!*

Chapter Two

Maddie's mom showed her some more photos of the kittens. Three were tabbies and the other two were tortoiseshells, beautiful black, white, and orange cats. They were all snuggled around each other and their mother, who was black like Shadow. Maddie was pretty sure she would like a tortoiseshell – Tiger and Tom had turned her off from tabby cats.

"When can I see them?" Maddie asked the next morning at breakfast.

Mom smiled. "I've arranged for us to visit them today. And if you're sure which kitten you'd like, you can even bring it home! We can go to the pet store on the way to Donna's house to get everything we'll need."

As it turned out, they needed a lot of things. Maddie knew they would need a basket. And food and water bowls. But there was so much else. A collar. Grooming brush. Food. Special treats that were good for cleaning kitten teeth. Toys….

They were just about to go and pay for everything when Mom stopped. "Oh, I forgot that Donna said we needed to bring a cat carrier to take the kitten home."

Maddie smiled. *Home!* She loved the idea of their house being a home for a kitten.

"If you get anything else, we won't have room for the kitten in the car," Dad muttered, but Maddie knew he was only joking.

"Can we go to Donna's now?" she said hopefully, as they loaded all the things in the trunk a few minutes later.

Mom nodded, and hugged her. "I'm really excited."

Maddie threw her arms around her mom's neck. "I bet I'm more excited than you."

Dad got in the car and blew the horn at them. "Come on. I'm so excited I actually want to go and see these kittens sometime today!"

"Oh, look at them!" Maddie breathed, stopping in the kitchen doorway. The kittens were asleep in a large basket in the corner of the room. It was by the radiator, and the floor had been covered with newspaper.

"They're doing pretty well with their house-training; the newspaper's just in case they miss the litter box," Donna explained. "We've been keeping them in the kitchen up until now, but this past week they've been escaping!"

"How old are they?" Maddie asked. They looked so little. She couldn't believe they were ready to leave their mom.

"Ten weeks yesterday. I bought a book about raising kittens when we found out that Dilly was pregnant, and it recommended keeping them with their mom until then, so she can teach them what they need to know. Also, that way they get to spend more time with their brothers and sisters, and learn how to get along."

"So did you mean for her to have kittens then?" Maddie's dad asked.

Donna sighed. "No, it was a total surprise. We were planning to have Dilly spayed, but it was too late. As soon as she's recovered from having these, we'll take her to the vet. I love the kittens, but I don't want more!"

"Are you going to keep any of them?" Maddie asked, as she knelt down by the basket. "They're so beautiful."

Donna nodded. "I know. I'd love to keep a couple, and it will be sad for Dilly to lose them all, but we only ever meant to have one cat! We'll have to see. Many people seem interested in adopting one." She smiled at Maddie. "But you've got first choice. Your mom saved you a kitten weeks ago!"

Maddie looked up at her mom gratefully. "Thanks, Mom!"

"Well, it seemed like a perfect opportunity – you're old enough to help take care of a pet now."

"I'll be really good, I promise," Maddie said. "I'll even clean the litter box." She wouldn't mind, she thought, peering into the basket. The kittens had heard their voices, and were starting to wake up. Dilly was watching Maddie carefully, obviously guarding her babies.

One of the tabby kittens popped its head up and stared curiously at Maddie. She laughed, and his eyes widened in surprise.

"Oh, sorry!" Maddie whispered. "I didn't mean to scare you."

All the kittens were awake now, gazing at her with big green eyes. Maddie sighed. "How am I ever going to choose one of you?" she said. She didn't think she wanted a tabby kitten, but they were cute, too – their pink noses clashed with their orange fur.

One of the tortoiseshell kittens put its paws up on the side of the basket, and nosed at Maddie's hand. Its nose felt chilly and tickly, and Maddie stifled a laugh. She didn't want to make the kitten jump.

"Is this a girl kitten?" she whispered to Donna. She'd guessed that the tabby kittens were boys and the tortoiseshells were girls, but she knew it wasn't always the case.

"Yes. She's a sweetie. Very friendly. She loves to have her head petted."

The kitten looked at Maddie hopefully, and Maddie gently rubbed the top of her head. Maddie smiled. The kitten purred, and turned her head sideways, nestling into Maddie's hand.

"She's pretty," Mom said quietly.

"Can we take her?" Maddie breathed. The kitten was still purring and cuddling up against Maddie's hand. She was so little and perfect. Maddie was desperate to pick her up, but she wasn't sure she should.

The kitten solved the problem by clambering over the side of the basket – it was a soft, squashy one, and the sides were so high that she looked like she was trying to climb over a bouncy castle. There was a lot of scrambling, but eventually she landed on the floor, looking very proud of herself, and started climbing onto Maddie's lap.

"Oooh, claws." Maddie giggled, and gently put her hand under the kitten's bottom to help her up. The kitten finally reached Maddie's lap, looking worn out by the effort, but she purred delightedly when Maddie petted her fur.

"Well, it looks like she wants to be ours, too," Dad said, reaching out a finger to scratch behind the kitten's ears. "What are we going to name her?"

Maddie looked down at the kitten, who was busily curling herself into a neat little ball. "See that dark patch on her back? It's completely round. Don't you think it looks just like a cookie?"

"Cookie?" Mom laughed. "That's a really cute name for a cat. It does look like a little chocolate cookie against that white fur."

Maddie nodded. "It's the perfect name for her."

Maddie had the rest of the Easter vacation to get to know Cookie, and play with her. Her mom and dad were right – having her kitten did mean she spent less time worrying about going back to school without Kate. She also did a lot of reading – they'd bought a book on cat care at the pet store, and she took a couple more out of the library, too.

"Did Donna take the kittens to have their first vaccinations?" she asked Mom at breakfast, the day after they'd brought Cookie home.

Cookie was sitting on Maddie's lap, looking hopefully at Maddie's breakfast. The cereal looked just like her cat treats, she thought, but it didn't smell the same. She reached up, and sniffed harder. Definitely not cat treats, but a very good smell all the same. She put her front paws on the edge of the table, and darted her raspberry-pink tongue toward a drop of milk that Maddie had spilled.

It was sweet and cold, and Cookie gave a delighted little shiver. Maddie was looking at her cat book and didn't notice when Cookie edged forward, and stuck her tongue in the bowl to lap up the leftover cereal. She managed to get a few mouthfuls before Maddie spotted her.

"Cookie! You shouldn't be eating that! Oh, Mom, look! She has milk all over her whiskers!"

Cookie settled back on to Maddie's lap, licking her whiskers happily. She liked her food better, but it was nice to have a change....

"Oh, dear! I suppose a little bit won't do her any harm. You're done, aren't you? And yes, Donna gave us the vaccination certificate." Mom looked in the folder she'd left on the countertop. "She had them done about three weeks ago."

Maddie checked the book again. "Then we need to take her to the vet soon! She's supposed to have the second vaccination three weeks after the first one. And then in another three weeks, she'll be allowed to go outside."

"Actually, yes, that's what Donna's put in this note. She said we should probably have Cookie microchipped at the same time."

Maddie nodded. The tiny microchip went under the skin on the kitten's neck, and it would have a special number on it, so that Cookie could be easily identified by any vet if she got lost.

"I'll call the vet tomorrow," Mom said. "They're not open on Sunday."

Maddie nodded. "That reminds me! Can I call Kate, Mom? I have to tell her about Cookie!"

Luckily, the vet had a cancelled appointment on Monday afternoon. Maddie wanted to get Cookie's vaccinations done as soon as possible, so that she would be able to play with her in the yard. She knew that the little cat would love it. She was so adventurous inside the house. She kept climbing things, and she loved to tunnel under Maddie's comforter and then pop out at her.

For the trip to the vet, Maddie put the cat carrier next to her on the back seat, and Cookie peered out at her worriedly. She had only been in the cat carrier once, and that was to come to Maddie's house. Were they going back to her old home again? She did miss playing with her brothers and sisters, but Maddie was just as much fun to play with – and she didn't jump on her and try to chew her ears, like her big brother had done. Cookie definitely preferred Maddie's house. She let out a wail as Maddie lifted the carrier out of the car – but then she realized that it wasn't her old home they'd come to after all.

The place smelled very odd – sharp and chemical to her sensitive nose.

But at the same time, it was slightly familiar. Had she been here before?

Maddie put the carrier down on the floor, and Cookie sniffed suspiciously. There were other smells, too. A strange, worrying smell. It smelled like a dog. A dog had visited her old home once, and she hadn't liked it. She shifted nervously inside her carrier. It was coming closer!

Cookie gave a horrified squeak as a furry face loomed up in front of her carrier. The puppy peered in curiously and nudged the wire door with his nose.

The kitten bristled, her fur standing

on end and her tail fluffing up to twice its size. She hissed furiously at the dog. This was *her* carrier! She swiped her claws at his nose, but they scraped harmlessly down the wire.

"Barney, no!" his owner cried. "Oh, I'm so sorry. I hope he didn't scare your kitten."

Maddie's mom laughed. "Actually, I think she tried to fight back. She's a determined little thing."

Maddie looked anxiously into Cookie's carrier. "Are you all right? Sorry, Cookie, I was helping Mom fill out the forms. I didn't see what was happening." Then she smiled. Cookie was sitting in the carrier with her tail wrapped smugly around her. She wasn't afraid of some silly dog!

Chapter Three

"She's going to miss me while I'm at school," Maddie said worriedly. She had her coat and her backpack and her lunchbag – and a kitten sitting on her shoulder, sniffing with interest at the backpack. "It's the first day I won't get to play with her."

"I'll be here though," her mom replied. Maddie's mom worked

part-time at another school, but she didn't go in on Mondays or Fridays. "I'll play with her a lot, Maddie, I promise. And your dad's working from home tomorrow. Cookie will get used to being left alone. It'll be fine."

Maddie nodded doubtfully. She'd spent the entire vacation playing with Cookie and making a big deal about her. She just couldn't imagine a whole day at school without seeing her. And without Kate....

"Come on, Maddie. We'd better go."

Maddie sighed and then carefully unhooked Cookie's claws from her coat. She put her down gently and rubbed her ears. "Be good," she told her. "I'll be back soon."

Cookie stared up at her. She didn't

understand what was happening, but she could tell from Maddie's voice that she wasn't happy. The kitten gave an uncertain little meow and patted at Maddie's leg with a paw, asking to be picked up again.

"Maddie, now," her mom said firmly, seeing that Maddie was close to tears. She shooed her out of the door, leaving Cookie all alone in the house.

Cookie sat by the front door for a little while, hoping that they'd come back, but she couldn't hear any footsteps heading up the path. She didn't understand why Maddie left. Eventually, she padded back into the kitchen. She had seen Maddie and her mom and dad use the back door, even though she wasn't allowed out of it yet. Perhaps they would come in that way?

Cookie waited for what seemed like a very long time, but no one came in by that door, either. So she wandered through the house, meowing. Where had they all gone? Were they ever coming back? She looked at the stairs for a while, but she still found them very difficult to climb. Maddie had carried her up there a couple of times, but it took her a long time to get up the entire flight of stairs by herself.

Sadly, she trailed into the living room, and clawed her way up the purple blanket on the sofa. It already had quite a few claw marks on. Cookie had quickly discovered that the back of the sofa was an interesting place to sit. She sat down, peering out of the window, hoping to see Maddie coming up the front path.

Instead, she saw a large furry face staring back at her.

Cookie was so surprised that she jumped backward with a meow of fright, and fell onto the sofa.

What was that? Another cat? In her yard? Cookie had never been out in it, but she was sure that it was hers. She sat shivering on the sofa, not daring to climb up and look again. The other cat had been a lot bigger than she was. What if it was still there? At last, Cookie scrambled up the blanket again, and peeked over the back of the sofa.

The big tabby cat was gone.

Cookie was so relieved that she curled up on the back of the sofa and went to sleep.

"She was fine, Maddie!" Mom said, as they walked home from school. "When I got home from dropping you off and doing the shopping, she was asleep on the back of the sofa. And then the rest of the day I played with her every so often, and she was perfectly all right."

Maddie nodded, looking relieved. "I wonder if she was watching for us coming home, and that's why she was on the back of the sofa."

"Maybe." Her mom laughed. "Actually, I think she's just nosy. She likes watching people go past. Anyway, how was school?"

Maddie could tell that her mom was trying not to sound worried about her. She shrugged. "Okay."

"Who did you sit with?"

"Lucy. And Riley."

"And it was all right?"

Maddie didn't want to tell her mom that she'd felt miserable and lonely all day, and that even though Lucy and Riley had been nice, she'd hardly talked to them. She couldn't help thinking that they were Kate's friends, not hers, and they didn't really want to hang around with her. Luckily, there had been a kickball game at lunch, so she hadn't had to hang around on her own in the playground. But there wasn't a game every lunchtime. She sped up, hurrying home to see Cookie.

"Oh, look, she's there. Watching for us!" Maddie beamed. She ran up the path, watching Cookie leap off the back of the sofa. She could hear a little scuttle of paws, and then frantic meowing and a scratching noise as the kitten clawed at the door. As soon as her mom opened it, Maddie swept the kitten up to hug her.

School wasn't any easier the next day, or the day after that – but at least Maddie had Cookie to cheer her up at home. And she was really looking forward to Saturday – the vet had said Cookie could go out in the yard then, even though it wasn't quite three weeks since her shots. He'd said it would be fine as long as she wasn't around any other cats.

Maddie didn't give Cookie as much breakfast as usual on Saturday. And just in case Cookie did wander too far, Maddie made sure she had a full bag of the kitten's favorite chicken treats.

Cookie was still staring suspiciously at her food bowl, wondering why breakfast hadn't seemed to take as long to gobble down as usual, when she realized that the back door was wide open. She'd seen it open before, of course, but only when someone was holding her tightly, and even then it always slammed shut before she could wriggle free and go investigating. She crept over to it, keeping low to the ground, expecting any minute that Maddie or her mom would catch her.

But Maddie was outside! She was standing by the door, calling her! Cookie hurried so fast out the door that she almost tripped over the step. She shook herself angrily and pattered down the path to where Maddie was.

There were so many smells! She sniffed curiously at the grass, and patted it with one paw. It was cool and damp, and taller than she was!

"Do you have the treats?" Her mom appeared in the doorway. "In case Cookie goes running off. Remember, she could get under the fence if she really tried."

Maddie waved the foil packet. "It's okay. Oh, look! She saw a butterfly!"

The orange butterfly was swooping carelessly past Cookie's nose, and the kitten watched it in amazement. Maddie had dangled pieces of string for her, and feathery toys, but she had never seen anything like this. She reached out her paw and tried to bat at the butterfly, but it flew behind her, and she almost fell over trying to chase after it.

"You can't have it, Cookie," Maddie laughed. "I don't think butterflies are

very good for you. And they're all legs
and wings; I bet they don't taste good."

Cookie stared after the butterfly,
which was flittering over the fence to
the yard next door. She thought
it looked delicious. But there
was no way she could get
over the high fence to
follow it.

Chapter Four

Maddie and Cookie spent so much time playing in the yard that on Friday evening, Maddie's dad came home with a surprise. He put the big box he was carrying down in front of Cookie's cat basket.

"What is it?" Maddie asked, looking at the front of the box. Cookie blinked at it sleepily. She was worn out from running around the yard with Maddie after Maddie had gotten home from school.

"Oh, a cat flap! Thanks, Dad!"

"We can put it in tomorrow. It's been more than three weeks since Cookie had her vaccinations now, so we can let her out on her own."

Maddie nodded. "I guess so. But she's not even 14 weeks old. She's still so little."

"I think cats like to explore, though," Dad pointed out. "She'll be able to climb trees. Chase more butterflies...."

Cookie suddenly perked up, bouncing up and staring at him, ears pricked. Dad laughed. "You see?"

Maddie had been worried that Cookie might not be able to open the cat flap, or that she just might not like it – Kate had told her that it had taken Shadow a while to get used to his. But as soon as Cookie understood what the cat flap did, she took to it immediately. She spent most of Saturday afternoon popping in and out of it, coming back into the kitchen every five minutes to make sure that Maddie was still there.

Maddie had been nervous that Cookie might try leaving the yard. But even though Cookie had sniffed at the holes under the fence, there was plenty in Maddie's yard to keep her busy.

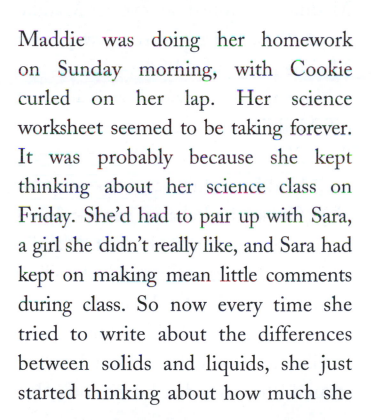

Maddie was doing her homework on Sunday morning, with Cookie curled on her lap. Her science worksheet seemed to be taking forever. It was probably because she kept thinking about her science class on Friday. She'd had to pair up with Sara, a girl she didn't really like, and Sara had kept on making mean little comments during class. So now every time she tried to write about the differences between solids and liquids, she just started thinking about how much she missed having Kate to work with. Kate would have said something funny about Sara, Maddie was sure.

At least Maddie saw that Becky, one of the girls who sat at the table behind Maddie, had rolled her eyes at Maddie in an "Ignore her!" sort of way, and Maddie had smiled back.

Now Cookie yawned and jumped off Maddie's lap, heading for her cat flap. She was bored with sitting still, and Maddie didn't seem to want to play. Cookie had chased some colored pencils across the table, but Maddie had put them away instead of rolling the pencils for her to chase.

The yard was full of interesting smells, and some bees were buzzing around the lavender bushes. Cookie watched them, fascinated, her tail tip twitching. She was watching so closely that she didn't see Tiger and Tom sneaking under the fence next door. It wasn't until the two big cats were right behind her that Cookie heard them creeping through the grass, and whirled around. She was sure it was one of these cats who'd been staring in at her through the window.

The tabby cats had their ears laid back as they snuck toward her. Cookie backed away from them into the lavender bush. She knew the two cats weren't friendly. Her tail bushed out, and she threw a nervous glance toward the door. Could she make a run for her cat flap? But one of the bigger tabby cats, the one with the torn ear, was between her and the house, his tail swishing from side to side.

Tiger, the one with the darker stripes, was almost nose to nose with her now, hissing and staring. Cookie was squashed into the lavender bush – she couldn't go back any further.

Tiger slapped her on the head with one enormous paw, sending her rolling, and Cookie wailed miserably. What was she supposed to do? Why were they attacking her?

Inside the house, Maddie was still gloomily eyeing her homework. She glanced up as her mom came into the kitchen, looking confused.

"Maddie, can you hear a strange noise? It almost sounds like a baby crying. A sort of howling."

Maddie yelped and suddenly pushed her chair away from the kitchen table, racing as fast as she could for the back door. She was sure it was Cookie.

She flung open the door, and Tom jumped, hissing at her, but Tiger and Cookie hardly seemed to notice. They were in the middle of the lawn now, and Tiger was about three times the size of Cookie with all his fur fluffed up. They were making all kinds of strange noises still, circling around each other. As Maddie watched, Tiger leaped on Cookie again, and the two cats seemed to roll over and over, twisting and scratching.

"Stop it!" Maddie yelled. She raced over to them, shoving Tiger, ignoring the hissing and scratching at her hands. She snatched Cookie up, and yelled at Tiger and Tom, sending them scurrying away under the fence.

"Maddie, are you all right?" Her mom came running out. "It all happened so quickly. I didn't realize what was going on. Is Cookie hurt?"

"I don't think so, but she's shaking." Maddie carried the kitten inside. "Those horrible cats!"

Her mom sighed. "I suppose they're used to coming into our yard. They think Cookie's in their territory."

"Well, she isn't!" Maddie snapped. "It's our yard and our cat!"

"Yes, we know that, but I bet the cats don't. Give her to me. You need to wash your hands. They must hurt. You're all scratched!"

Reluctantly, Maddie handed Cookie over to her mom.

"She's so scared," Maddie said, her

voice shaking. "Tiger's so much bigger than Cookie. He could have really hurt her." Then she laughed a little. "I saw Cookie scratch his nose, though, before he ran off."

"Did they go under the fence?" her mom asked. "Is there a hole we could block up?"

Maddie dried her scratched hands. "I'll go and see."

Cookie gave a worried little meow as she saw Maddie open the door, and Maddie stopped to pet her. "Don't worry. I'm not going to let those big cats anywhere near you."

She hurried out into the yard, checking the fence. There were holes all the way down the fence – big enough for a cat to squeeze through. It was going to be difficult to block them all up. And the fence wasn't that high, either. She was pretty sure that Tiger and Tom could climb it without too much effort.

"What are you doing?" someone asked in a snippy sort of voice.

Maddie stood up next to the flower bed. It was her neighbor, Josh, who owned Tiger and Tom. He was a couple of years older than she was and went to high school, so usually Maddie was too shy to say much to him. But not today.

"I'm looking at the fence! Your cats just came into my yard and attacked my kitten!" she snapped at him.

Josh shrugged. "Sorry. But cats fight. It's what they do."

"Don't you care? She's terrified!"

"There's nothing I can do. Cats chase each other and they fight. There are a lot of cats around here. Your kitten's going to get into fights, Maddie. Stop being such a girl."

"OH!" Maddie huffed, and she stomped back inside. Cookie was not going to fight, because Maddie wasn't going to let any other cats hurt her. Maddie didn't care how scratched *she* got.

But as she shut the kitchen door, slamming it hard enough to set the cat flap swinging, Maddie had a sudden, awful thought.

She could protect Cookie now, but what about tomorrow, when she went back to school?

"Maybe we shouldn't have gotten a cat flap," Maddie said worriedly.

Her dad scratched his head thoughtfully. He hadn't been home when Cookie got into the fight, and had missed the whole thing. "I can't exactly put that chunk of door back.

Anyway, Cookie's getting bigger all the time. She won't be such an easy target for those cats next door soon."

"I don't think Cookie's ever going to be as big as they are," Maddie said. "But it's good for her to be able to go out. She loves being in the yard! Or she did, anyway," she added sadly.

Cookie hadn't been outside again since the fight that morning. She'd retreated into the dining room. There was a nice patch of warm sun coming through the glass doors at the back of the room. Cookie lay in it, feeling the soft warmth on her fur. It made her feel better – not so jumpy and scared.

She stretched out on the carpet lazily and gazed out of the big window through half-open eyes, hoping to see some butterflies.

Instead, the next time she blinked, Tiger and Tom were there. In her yard, staring at her, just on the other side of the window.

Cookie's tail fluffed up, and she hissed in panic. For a moment, she forgot that there was glass there and they couldn't reach her through it. She was sure that Tiger was about to knock her over again. She raced out to the kitchen and Maddie, meowing in fright.

"They're back!" Maddie picked Cookie up, cuddling her.

Dad quickly filled up a glass that was by the sink and headed out into the yard. But he came back shaking his head. "I was going to splash them – cats don't like getting wet – but they were gone already."

"If they keep doing this, Cookie's going to be frightened all the time," Maddie said anxiously. "It's so unfair."

She was still worrying when she went to bed that night. She'd left the kitten snoozing in her basket in the kitchen, after putting some of Cookie's favorite cat treats in her bowl, in case she woke up needing a midnight snack.

It took Maddie a long time to get to sleep. She tossed and turned, thinking about Tiger and Tom, and then about school tomorrow. Somehow her thoughts all got mixed together so that she was sitting in math class with Tiger and Tom (in the school uniform) on either side of her. Tiger was just telling her that she'd gotten her multiplication wrong, when Tom started howling in her ear. Maddie twitched, turned over – and woke up. That awful noise wasn't in her dream – the sound was coming from downstairs!

She flung herself out of bed and dashed down the stairs. The noise was louder now, and it was coming from the kitchen. Maddie couldn't understand – it sounded like more than one cat, but only Cookie was supposed to be in there. She shoved open the door, and saw Tiger and Tom by Cookie's food bowl, gobbling down the cat treats that she'd left out.

"Go away!" Maddie yelled. "Out! Bad cats!" Tiger and Tom hissed at her, but hightailed it out of the cat flap. The cat flap – of course. That's how they'd got into Maddie's kitchen!

"What on earth…?" Dad appeared in the kitchen doorway, looking sleepy.

"The cats from next door came in through the cat flap, Dad; they were eating Cookie's food!" Maddie crouched down by Cookie's bed. The kitten looked terrified, and as Maddie gently picked her up, she could feel how tense Cookie was, ready to leap out of Maddie's arms and run away at any moment. Her whiskers were twitching, and her little eyes were huge.

Mom had been worried that Cookie might end up making a mess in Maddie's room if she slept upstairs, but Maddie couldn't bear the thought of leaving Cookie on her own.

"Dad, please can I take Cookie upstairs to sleep with me?" she begged. "I know Mom said she should stay in the kitchen, but she's so scared."

Dad sighed. "Well, she is house-trained now. And she's pretty good on the stairs, too. She'll be okay to come down if she needs her litter box. I'm going to put a chair in front of the cat flap in case Tiger and Tom come back."

Maddie nodded. Cookie was relaxing a little now, but she was still looking around nervously. Maddie hurried upstairs and fluffed up her comforter into a cozy kitten nest at the end of the bed. It didn't leave much comforter for her, but she didn't mind.

Cookie stepped into the warm nest and padded at it with her paws. Maddie was here. She was safe. Tiger and Tom wouldn't be able to come upstairs. And if they did, Maddie would chase them away.

Maddie slipped into bed. She'd wanted Cookie to sleep on her bed since she'd gotten the kitten, but she wished it hadn't happened like this.

Maddie was just falling asleep again when she felt little paws padding up her tummy, and a soft wisp of fur brushed across her cheek as Cookie curled up on the pillow. Maddie giggled. Cookie's tail was lying on Maddie's neck and it tickled.

"We'll figure out what to do," she told Cookie sleepily. "It'll be okay."

Chapter Five

"Time to get up!" Maddie's mom pulled open the bedroom curtains.

"Mmmm. Oh!" Maddie suddenly remembered that Cookie was upstairs with her, although Cookie wasn't asleep on her pillow anymore.

"Dad told me he'd let you bring Cookie up here. I guess it's fine, as long as you make sure she doesn't get shut in. We don't want her peeing on your bedroom carpet!" She looked around. "Where is she? Did she go downstairs already?"

Maddie sat up quickly. "She was sleeping next to me."

"She's here!" Her mom was crouching down, peering under the bed. "It's all right, Cookie. I'm not scary. Oh dear, Maddie; she looks very nervous."

"Maybe she heard you coming in and thought it was Tiger and Tom again." Maddie hopped out of bed to look underneath.

Cookie was squeezed as far back as she could go, pressed against the wall. Maddie saw her whiskers trembling. "Cookie! Come on, it's okay."

Slowly, Cookie crept out. Maddie picked her up, but she flinched when Maddie's mom tried to pet her.

"She's usually so friendly," Maddie's mom said sadly. "Maybe she'll feel better after some food."

"I hope so." Maddie carried Cookie downstairs with her once she'd gotten dressed. She could feel Cookie tensing up as they came down the hall into the kitchen. She was practically clinging on to Maddie's sweater, and she didn't seem very interested in eating even when Maddie filled up her bowl.

"Don't worry. I'll keep an eye on her while you're at school," Mom said. "How are things going, anyway?"

Maddie shrugged.

"I know you miss Kate, but I'm sure there are lots of other people in your class that you could talk to," her mom said persuasively.

But none of them is as nice as Kate, Maddie thought. *And no one wants to talk to me. It's just not that easy....*

"It's a month until Field Day," said Mrs. Melling, Maddie's teacher, as she led everyone out on to the school field. "So we're going to practice long-distance running, relay races, hurdles, that sort of thing."

Several people sighed grumpily, but Maddie smiled. She loved to run. And she was pretty good at it, too. She'd been worrying about Cookie all morning, even though Dad had blocked the cat flap in case Tiger and Tom tried to get in again. Maddie knew Cookie should be just fine, but she couldn't stop thinking about Cookie, and how frightened she'd been. Maddie hoped that some running in the warm sun would shake off the jittery, miserable feeling inside her.

The field had an oval track painted on to the grass, and after they warmed up, Mrs. Melling divided them into groups to run heats. Maddie won her first heat easily – none of the others was really trying – but she was surprised when she beat a couple of boys in the next race. Some of the girls even started cheering for her at the end.

"Great job! You're so quick!" Becky came over and patted her on the back.

Maddie laughed nervously. She'd always liked Becky, but Becky was popular and had lots of friends. She was nice to Maddie, but they'd never hung around together much.

"Beat Joe in this last race, please!" Becky begged. "He's so full of himself. Look at him!"

Joe was talking to the other boys and doing show-off stretches. He obviously thought he was going to win.

"Okay." Maddie grinned. She wasn't tired at all. As they lined up for the last race, she bounced on her toes, staring at the finish line. As soon as Mrs. Melling blew her whistle, Maddie shot away, sprinting as fast as she could, and crossed the finish line just ahead of Joe.

"Yay! Maddie won!" She could hear Becky yelling above all the others. It felt fantastic.

With Becky and the others hugging her and telling her she was a star, it was easy to laugh off Joe growling about girls always cheating. And Becky's table in class was behind hers, so Maddie could see Becky grinning at her every so often as they had reading after PE. It was the best time she'd had in school all quarter. She couldn't wait to tell her mom and dad about it. They kept asking how school was going, and it would be nice to be able to say she'd had a fun day.

"How was Cookie?" Maddie asked hopefully, as she rushed up to her mom after school.

Mom made a face. "She's been scratching the sofa! I had to keep her out of the living room."

"Oh…." Maddie frowned. Cookie had never done that before. She hoped mom wasn't too angry.

When they got home, Maddie put her bags down, expecting the kitten to bounce up to her, wanting to play, like she usually did. But Cookie didn't come running.

"Cookie!" Maddie looked around anxiously.

"Try upstairs," her mom suggested. "She seems to like it there now."

Maddie ran up to her room. She couldn't see Cookie, but she had a horrible feeling she knew where the kitten was. Maddie knelt down, looking under the bed. She was right. Cookie was curled up in the corner again, looking at her with wide, worried eyes.

"Oh, Cookie," Maddie whispered. "It's all right, sweetie, come on out."

"I don't think we can keep the cat flap blocked," Dad said, looking down at his ice cream thoughtfully. "Cookie needs to be able to go out."

"But she doesn't want to," Maddie explained. "She's scared."

"It isn't good to keep her in. She should be sharpening her claws on trees, not the sofa," Mom sighed.

"And it would be nice not to have to keep cleaning out the litter box!"

"I'll do it," Maddie said quickly. "I don't mind. She's too scared to go in the yard."

She licked ice cream off her spoon, but she wasn't really hungry anymore. She could feel Mom and Dad both looking at her. And she was pretty sure they thought she was worrying too much.

"I think Cookie might just need to toughen up a bit," Dad said gently.

"She's definitely getting bigger," Mom pointed out. "She'll be as big as Tiger and Tom soon."

"I bet she won't," Maddie said. "And however big she is, there's still only one of her. Tiger and Tom work as a team, Mom! Like wrestlers!"

Her mom frowned and glanced meaningfully at her dad. Maddie knew what that look meant. They thought she was upset about Cookie because of school. Because she was feeling nervous and worried, too. Mom and Dad reckoned Maddie needed to make some new friends.

"I'll see if I can find some ideas," she said quickly, wanting to get away before they started asking about school again, and if there was anyone she wanted to invite over to play. *Maybe I could ask Becky over*, she thought, and then crushed the idea firmly. Becky was much too popular to want to hang around with her.

"You want to do what?" Josh made a snorting noise.

"Take turns," Maddie repeated, wriggling to keep her elbows on top of the fence. She was standing on a bucket to see over the fence, and it was a bit wobbly. "You keep Tiger and Tom in some of the time, so Cookie can go out without them scaring her."

After a snack, she'd searched her favorite pet advice websites, and found an email waiting for her from Kate. Maddie had sent her a message a couple of days ago, asking if she had any advice. The turn-taking idea was something Kate had read about once, and it sounded perfect.

Maddie took a deep breath. She didn't like talking to Josh; he always made her feel silly. But she had to. "Please can you think about it? Cookie is getting really twitchy and nervous. It wouldn't have to be long. Maybe only for an hour a day? Just until she's bigger and can stand up for herself."

Josh shrugged. "How am I supposed to keep them in? Tiger and Tom have a cat flap. They go in and out whenever they want to."

"But couldn't you—" Maddie began.

"I've got football. I need to go," Josh interrupted. And he disappeared through his back door, leaving Maddie peering after him.

Maddie sighed. Taking turns had seemed like such a good idea. Except that Josh couldn't be bothered!

She trailed back into the kitchen and found Cookie sitting on one of the chairs, staring anxiously at the cat flap – Maddie had moved the chair blocking it so she could get out.

"We'll have to think of something else," she told Cookie, tickling her under the chin.

Cookie rubbed her head against Maddie's hand and purred.

She really trusts me, Maddie thought. *I have to figure this out.*

Chapter Six

Cookie didn't go out on her own at all for the rest of the week. Maddie took her out into the yard a few times, since she was pretty sure Tiger and Tom wouldn't come into the yard if Maddie was there. But as soon as she put Cookie down, the kitten would race for her cat flap. And even when she was inside, she spent most of her time hiding under Maddie's bed. She even peed on the floor, which made Mom angry.

"I know it isn't her fault, Maddie," mom told her as she scrubbed the carpet. "But the smell is horrible!"

"You don't want us to give her back to Donna, do you?" Maddie asked anxiously.

Mom shook her head. "No. But we need to figure this out. Anyway, we'd better get going to school now."

Cookie watched them from under the bathroom towel rack. She liked it there. It was warm and dark, and the bathroom didn't have any windows to see other cats. She hadn't gone downstairs to eat yet. She just wasn't sure she was brave enough. What if

Tiger and Tom came back into the kitchen again?

As the front door banged behind Maddie, Cookie crept to the top of the stairs. She was so hungry that she would have to risk going to the kitchen. She hurried down the stairs and peered around the kitchen door. No sign of any strange cats. Gratefully, she hurried in and started to gulp down her food, stopping every few seconds to glance around worriedly.

When she had eaten about half of her food, she began to relax a little to enjoy the meal.

Then the front door banged and she leaped away from the bowl in fright. Was it Tiger and Tom again?

Panicking, Cookie shot into the corner of the kitchen, trying to hide. She was so scared that she peed all over the floor.

"Oh, no! Cookie!" Maddie's mom said angrily, as she got back and saw the mess. "What on earth did you do that for? It's only me." She went to the cupboard under the sink to get some spray and a cloth. "Go on, shoo. I've got to clean this up." She flapped the cloth at Cookie grumpily.

Cookie was so jittery that the flash of white cloth scared her, and she shot out of the cat flap to get away from it. Maddie's mom had gone to get the mop, and she didn't notice that the kitten was gone.

Cookie sat on the back step, staring

around the yard. She hadn't been outside for a week, and there were so many tempting smells. And there were bees buzzing near the lavender bushes. And butterflies…. She padded out on to the lawn, feeling the warmth as the sun hit her fur.

She didn't even see Tiger before he leaped out from under the fence and spat at her. She turned to race for the cat flap, but he chased her, knocking her sideways and clawing her ear. Cookie looked around for Tom, wondering if he was about to jump out at her, too, but Tiger was on his own for once. Not that it mattered at all – he was still more than twice as big as she was and horribly fierce. Cookie meowed as Tiger pounced at her again.

She was never going to be able to get away. Unless…. She tried to scratch him, shooting out a sharp-clawed paw, and he retreated a little, hissing. It gave her time to think.

If she couldn't beat him running, maybe she could go over the fence? It was worth a try. She jumped at Tiger, clawing him again, and then raced past him, heading for the fence. She raced up it, scrambling and fighting for the top. Then she perched there, wobbling, and looked down at Tiger, who stared back up at her.

Cookie gave a frightened little squeak, then jumped off the other side of the fence....

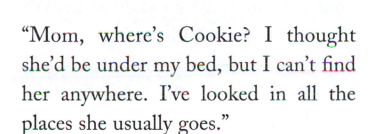

"Mom, where's Cookie? I thought she'd be under my bed, but I can't find her anywhere. I've looked in all the places she usually goes."

Mom frowned. "I haven't actually seen her much today. She peed on the kitchen floor this morning. But I'm not sure when I saw her after that. I had to go shopping, and then I came straight back from the store to pick you up."

Maddie looked at Cookie's bed, as if she might suddenly appear from underneath it. Then she noticed the cat flap. "Oh! You moved the chair!"

"I had to," Mom said grimly. "I was wiping up cat pee around it. I see what you mean, though. She might have gone out. But that's good, Maddie! We want her to go outside again."

"Not if those two cats are around," Maddie muttered. "I'm going to check outside for her."

But there was no sign of Cookie in the yard either, even after Maddie called and called.

"Did you find her?" her mom asked, leaning out the kitchen door. She was looking slightly worried now, too.

"No, and we usually feed her right about now."

"I'll look upstairs again. Maybe she got shut in somewhere," Mom said.

Maddie had already checked everywhere, but she nodded anyway. "Cookie! Cookie!" she called again.

"Did you lose your kitten?"

Maddie jumped. She hadn't realized Josh was out in his yard. "Yes. You haven't seen her, have you?"

"Nope."

"Could you watch for her? Please?" Maddie asked.

"Yeah, all right." But he didn't sound very convincing, Maddie thought.

She ran back inside. "Mom, do you think we should go and look for her? Oh, but we can't!"

"Why not?" Her mom looked confused.

"If your cat gets lost, it's best to leave someone familiar in the house — otherwise, the cat might not think it's the right home if it comes back. My book said so."

"Really? Okay, well, if she's not back when Dad gets home, you and I can go and look for her then."

The hour before Maddie's dad got home seemed to drag. Maddie kept searching the same places over and over, just in case she'd somehow missed Cookie all the times she'd checked earlier.

As soon as she saw her dad at the gate, Maddie was out of the front door and running down the path.

"Cookie's lost! We're going to look for her! Stay here!" she gasped.

Her dad stared at her, and then at Mom.

Maddie's mom looked at him worriedly. "I said we'll go and look around the streets. I don't think she could have gone far."

Maddie was already hurrying along, looking under parked cars. "Come on, Mom!" she called.

Cookie peered miserably out at the strange yard. She'd jumped off the fence, and trying to look behind her at the same time, she'd landed badly, injuring one of her front paws.

It hurt, and so did the scratches. But she'd kept going, desperate to get as far away from Tiger as she could. She'd crawled under fence after fence, hurrying on and on, until at last she felt as if she might be safe. She'd smelled several other cats and even seen a couple, but none of them had chased her yet.

Eventually she'd stopped to rest behind a yard shed. She didn't feel like she could go any further; her paw hurt so much. She'd huddled there for the rest of the day, unsure what to do. She couldn't go home, could she? Tiger would chase her again. She'd have to wait until she was sure Maddie was back; then it would be safe.

They searched for a long time. Maddie kept looking at the road and hoping that Cookie hadn't run out in front of a car. *I should have taken better care of her. I should have made Josh do something about Tiger and Tom,* she kept thinking. *When I find Cookie, I'm going to tell him!*

They were halfway down the next road and Maddie was hanging over a wall, staring into some tall flowers, when a surprised voice said, "What are you doing?"

Maddie jumped. She hadn't even

noticed anyone approaching. Becky from school was standing behind her, while her mom locked up the car. She was wearing a cardigan over ballet clothes, and peering over the wall to see what Maddie was looking at.

"Hi, Becky. I'm looking for my kitten." Maddie swallowed. "She's lost…." It was so horrible to say it.

"Oh, no! The cute little tortoiseshell one? You've got her picture in your locker, don't you?"

Maddie nodded. She was surprised Becky had noticed.

"Want me to help look? Can I, Mom? We were just coming back from ballet," Becky explained. "This is our house. I didn't know you lived so close to us."

Maddie blushed. "Sorry about looking in your yard," she said to Becky's mom.

"Don't worry," Becky's mom replied with a smile. "You can help Maddie look, Becky. But only until it's dark – you've probably got another half an hour, that's all."

Maddie looked around anxiously. Cookie had never even been out at night! She hated the thought of her being all alone in the dark.

The two girls went on up the road, calling for Cookie, and Becky's mom joined in, too, asking their neighbors if they'd seen a kitten. But no one had.

"We have to stop. It's too dark," Maddie's mom said eventually.

"We can't!" Maddie said pleadingly.

"I'll come and help you look first thing tomorrow," Becky told her, giving her a hug. "Don't worry. We'll find her."

As it was starting to get dark, Cookie decided she could leave her hiding place. Maddie must be home by now. As long as Cookie could get back in through her cat flap before Tiger spotted her, she would be safe.

She crawled out of the dark space behind the shed, wincing as she tried to put her weight on the hurt paw. It seemed to be getting worse. She limped across the yard, and squeezed under the fence, only to see a pair of glinting amber eyes, glaring at her from under a bush. She backed away nervously. Her first thought was that it was Tiger, but it didn't smell like him. It was a strange smell – strong and fierce. And the creature it belonged to was big….

The fox darted forward and snapped at her, his teeth huge and yellow.

Cookie ran blindly. She didn't know

where she was going – just away. She darted down a side path, under a gate and out on to the pavement, where she stopped and glanced quickly behind her. The fox wasn't following. But now she had even less of an idea where she was, and her paw was throbbing after her panicked dash. She limped on, hobbling down the curb. She needed to rest, and there was a yard on the other side of the road that looked like a good hiding place, overgrown, with bushes spilling over a low fence. Cookie set off across the road, not seeing the car turning the corner.

She was halfway across when she noticed it – the huge machine that seemed to be towering over her, its lights dazzling her. The car braked sharply, its tires squealing on the road. Cookie wailed as she dived forward out of the way, her injured paw collapsing underneath her, so that she half-dragged herself across the road. She struggled through the gate of the overgrown yard and flung herself down under the dark bushes, her breath coming in terrified gasps. She was so tired, and everything seemed to hurt.

Cookie lay there, gazing into the dark night. She had no idea where she was, or how to get back to Maddie. What was she going to do?

Chapter Seven

Becky's mom dropped her off first thing on Saturday morning. "It's not too early, is it?" Becky asked. "Mom said it might be, but I told her you'd want to get looking right away."

Maddie half-smiled. "I've been up for a while. I'm just waiting for Dad. It's really nice of you to come."

Becky shook her head. "I said

I would! I want to help you find her."

Maddie's dad appeared behind her. "Ready, girls?"

As they came out of the gate, Tiger and Tom prowled down Josh's front path and leaped onto the wall, staring at them with round green eyes.

Maddie clenched her fists. "Look at them! They're so mean!"

"Are they the ones who scared Cookie?" Becky asked. Maddie had told her how scared Cookie had been.

Maddie nodded. "They're horrible."

Becky pushed open Josh's gate, glaring at the cats. "Come on! Don't you think we should make Josh help us look?"

"I suppose so," Maddie faltered. She shook herself. "Yes, he should."

"Come on, then," said Maddie's dad.

Maddie stomped up the path and rang the doorbell. She was shocked when Josh's dad answered the front door. She'd been expecting Josh.

"Um…. We wondered…."

"Your cats chased her kitten away," Becky put in over Maddie's shoulder.

Maddie's dad nodded. "She's lost, I'm afraid. We haven't seen her since yesterday morning."

Josh's dad looked worried. "Josh did say something about Tiger and Tom having a fight with a new cat…."

Maddie nodded. "We think they had another fight, and she ran off."

"Oh, dear. Look, Josh has to go to his football game, but can we come and help you look afterward?"

"Thanks," Maddie told him, and the girls set off to search again.

Cookie twitched and wriggled in her sleep, then woke up with a jolt, her fur all on end. She stared around the thick bushes, searching for the strange creature that had been chasing her. It had been even bigger than Tiger and Tom. But the gloomy space under the branches was empty – just her and a few beetles. She'd only been dreaming.

She peered out from under the bushes into the overgrown yard, her whiskers twitching.

The house had been abandoned, and the yard was covered in brambles and weeds. Cookie shivered in the early morning chill. She was stiff all over. She wasn't used to sleeping outside. She hadn't meant to, either; she'd been planning to hurry home to Maddie. But the car had scared her so much, she'd crawled into this safe little hole and fallen into an exhausted sleep.

Now she had to get home. And Maddie would feed her, too. She was so hungry. It seemed like forever since she'd had anything to eat.

Cookie stood up, ready to creep out of her hiding place, but then she collapsed, meowing with pain as her paw seemed to double up underneath her. She tried again, putting her weight on her other front paw, but she could hardly move. Her injured paw was dragging painfully as she limped through the damp grass. She had to stop and rest every few steps, and her paw was hurting more and more now. Finally, Cookie sank down at the edge of the weedy gravel path. She couldn't go any further for a while.

She was frozen, her fur was soaked through from the dew, and she was aching all over.

How was she ever going to get home?

"If we don't find her soon, maybe we should make a poster." Becky said. They'd searched all down Maddie's road again, and gone around the park, and the maze of little streets between the park and school. Now they were going back down Becky's road.

Maddie swallowed. "Yes," she whispered. It made sense. They'd been searching all morning. But it seemed like admitting that Cookie was really lost. Lost Cat posters always made her so sad. She couldn't imagine seeing Cookie's photo stuck to posts and fences.

"Let's keep calling her for a little longer," she whispered. She rubbed her eyes to wipe away the tears, then shouted, "Cookie! Cookie!"

Curled up by the path, Cookie was startled out of her half-sleep. That was Maddie, she was sure! She struggled to get up, but she couldn't stand on her hurt leg at all now. What if Maddie didn't see her? The yard was so overgrown that Maddie might easily miss her. Cookie wailed desperately, a long, heartbroken meow.

On the other side of the road, Maddie stopped, almost bumping into Becky. "Did you hear that?"

"Yes! Do you think it was Cookie?"

Maddie's dad came running up the road. "Maddie, I think I heard—"

"I know! We did, too! Come on!" Grabbing Becky by the hand, Maddie hurried across the road. "It sounds like Cookie's in that yard!"

Becky nodded. "I think you're right. No one lives in that house anymore. It's really quiet. And spooky. I don't like walking past it. But it would be a good place to hide if she was scared."

Cookie could hear Maddie getting closer. She meowed desperately and wobbled down the path, dragging her useless leg.

"She's here!" Maddie flung the gate open. "Oh, Cookie, you're hurt! She can't walk, Dad."

"Did she get hit by a car?" Becky asked anxiously.

Maddie picked up Cookie, as gently

as she could. "I'm not sure. Her paw's hanging funny, but it's not bleeding. She's scratched, though, on her ears and nose. I knew Tiger and Tom had been after her again!"

"We'd better get her looked at by the vet," said Dad, taking out his phone.

Cookie lay on Maddie, purring faintly. Maddie had found her. Cookie rubbed her chin lovingly against Maddie's shirt. She wasn't leaving her, ever again.

Chapter Eight

"Is she going to be all right?" Maddie asked, exchanging an anxious look with Becky. Becky had begged to come to the vet; she was desperate to know if Cookie was going to be okay.

The vet nodded slowly. "I think she's just torn a muscle in her leg. She probably jumped and landed badly. She just needs to rest it. And I'll clean up these scratches and give her an injection of antibiotics, just in case. You said she's had trouble with the neighbor's cats? Looks like she's had a hard time."

Maddie nodded. "She won't go outside because she's so scared. They even came in through her cat flap. I'm not sure she feels safe even inside the house now."

The vet glanced at his computer screen. "She is microchipped, isn't she?"

"Yes, we had it done with her vaccinations," Dad said. "Why?"

"There's a new kind of cat flap you can get – it's a little expensive, but it works with the microchip. So only your cat would be able to use it."

Maddie looked at Dad hopefully. "Can I have one of those for my birthday, just a little early? Please?"

Dad was grinning. "Two months early? We might be able to do that."

"You can program it, too, so you can keep Cookie in at night, if you want," the vet added.

Maddie nodded. "Then if Josh and his dad agree to keep Tiger and Tom in some of the time, we could tell the cat flap only to let Cookie out when we know they're inside!"

"Was it two boys who were fighting her?" the vet asked. "Are they neutered? Boy cats can be rough, if they haven't been. It might be worth suggesting to their owner that he has that done for them."

"We'll talk to Josh's dad," Dad promised Maddie.

Maddie cradled Cookie in her lap. They'd gone to the vet in such a rush that they hadn't put her in the cat carrier.

"I'll drop you two off, and then I'll go and see if that big pet store by the supermarket has those special cat flaps," Dad said as he pulled in.

"Look, there's Josh and his dad!" Maddie got out, carrying Cookie.

"You found her!" Josh's dad hurried forward. "Is she okay?"

"She's hurt her paw, and we had to take her to the vet," Maddie explained.

"She's really scratched, too…." Josh's dad peered at Cookie's nose. "Was that our two?"

Maddie nodded. "I think so. Are Tiger and Tom neutered? The vet

119

said maybe that would help. He gave us a pamphlet with information."

Becky gave the pamphlet to Josh's dad's. "Probably not," he said. "We didn't have them fixed. They were strays. They showed up at work, about three years ago, and I brought them home. They were only tiny – about the size of your little one."

"Ohh...." Somehow, knowing that Tiger and Tom had been stray kittens made Maddie feel less angry with them. And Josh and his dad. It wasn't as if they'd asked to be cat owners, and they'd never realized how important it was to have the cats neutered.

"We can try and keep them in sometimes, too, like you said," Josh put in suddenly.

"That would be wonderful," Maddie said gratefully. She brushed her cheek lightly over Cookie's soft head. It was all going to be okay. She should call Kate to tell her what had happened. It was a nice thought. It didn't make her feel teary, like it would have done a couple of days ago. She missed Kate. But it wasn't as bad anymore, somehow....

"I guess I'd better get home," Becky said as they reached Maddie's.

"Can you stay for a little while?" Maddie asked. "That's okay, isn't it?"

she added to her mom, who had come out into the yard and was looking anxiously at Cookie. "It's good news, Mom. The vet says she probably just tore a muscle."

"Of course you can stay, Becky. Call your mom. Is Cookie really all right?" Maddie's mom petted Cookie gently. "Oh, she's purring."

Maddie beamed. "She is! She must be feeling better now that she's home."

"Maddie!"

Maddie looked around and saw Becky racing across the playground toward her. "How's Cookie?"

"Much better," Maddie said happily.

"She walking again now. She's has a little limp, but it's not too bad."

"I bet you're watching her like a hawk." Becky laughed.

"I love spoiling her," Maddie admitted. She looked at Becky shyly. "Mom said I could ask you over, so you can see how she is."

Becky beamed. "Really? Yes, please! Can I come today? Just to pop in and see her on the way home?"

"Yes, of course." Maddie could feel her face turn pink. She hadn't been sure if Becky would be as friendly at school as she had been over the weekend.

"Do you think Mrs. Melling would let you move tables, now that Kate isn't here anymore?" Becky asked thoughtfully. "There's space for you to sit with me and Lara and Keri."

"I guess we could ask," Maddie said, turning even more pink.

"Cool." Becky pulled her over to the small group of girls she'd been talking to. "Do you have a picture of Cookie in your bag to show everyone?"

"She looks different," Becky said thoughtfully later that afternoon, as the girls sat in Maddie's kitchen, watching Cookie sleeping in her basket.

"The scratches don't look as bad," Maddie suggested.

"No, it isn't that. I think she just looks happier. She must have been feeling miserable on Saturday." Becky glanced at the door. "Did your dad get that special cat flap?"

"Yes. And then he talked to Josh's dad about when Cookie gets to go outside. Josh's dad said that he called the vet, and Tiger and Tom are scheduled for Wednesday. Once they're neutered, the vet said he was sure they'd be less fierce."

"That's amazing." Becky grinned. "Aren't you glad I made you ring their bell? Oh, look! Cookie's awake!"

Cookie opened her eyes and yawned, showing her raspberry-pink tongue.

Then she looked lovingly at Maddie, and stepped out of her basket and on to Maddie's lap. She gave Becky a curious stare.

"Can I pet her?"

Maddie nodded. "She doesn't seem as jumpy as she did before. It can't really be the new cat flap, because she hasn't even been out yet."

"Maybe she's just glad to be home," Becky suggested.

Maddie smiled at Cookie. She seemed to be going back to sleep again, just on a warmer, cozier sort of bed.

Cookie burrowed deeper into Maddie's school sweater, and purred softly with each breath. She was safe now. And she wasn't frightened anymore.

HOLLY WEBB

Holly Webb started out as a children's book editor, and wrote her first series for the publisher she worked for. She has been writing ever since, with more than 90 books to her name. Holly lives in England with her husband and three young sons. She has three pet cats, who are always nosing around when Holly is trying to type on her laptop.

For more information about Holly Webb visit:

www.holly-webb.com
www.tigertalesbooks.com